Judy Moody & Stink

The WISHBONE WISH

Books about Judy Moody and Stink
by Megan McDonald, illustrated by Peter H. Reynolds

Judy Moody and Stink: The Holly Joliday
Judy Moody and Stink: The Mad, Mad, Mad, Mad Treasure Hunt
Judy Moody and Stink: The Big Bad Blackout

Judy Moody
Judy Moody Gets Famous!
Judy Moody Saves the World!
Judy Moody Predicts the Future
Judy Moody, M.D.: The Doctor Is In!
Judy Moody Declares Independence
Judy Moody Around the World in 8½ Days
Judy Moody Goes to College
Judy Moody, Girl Detective
Judy Moody and the NOT Bummer Summer
Judy Moody and the Bad Luck Charm
Judy Moody, Mood Martian
Judy Moody and the Bucket List

Stink: The Incredible Shrinking Kid
Stink and the Incredible Super-Galactic Jawbreaker
Stink and the World's Worst Super-Stinky Sneakers
Stink and the Great Guinea Pig Express
Stink: Solar System Superhero
Stink and the Ultimate Thumb-Wrestling Smackdown
Stink and the Midnight Zombie Walk
Stink and the Freaky Frog Freakout
Stink and the Shark Sleepover
Stink and the Attack of the Slime Mold

Judy Moody & Stink
The WISHBONE WISH

Megan McDonald
illustrated by Peter H. Reynolds

CANDLEWICK PRESS

This is a work of fiction. Names, characters, places, and incidents are either products of the author's imagination or, if real, are used fictitiously.

First paperback edition 2016

Library of Congress Catalog Card Number 2014949723
ISBN 978-0-7636-7206-5 (hardcover)
ISBN 978-0-7636-9099-1 (paperback)

16 17 18 19 20 21 CCP 10 9 8 7 6 5 4 3 2 1

Printed in Shenzhen, Guangdong, China

MIX
Paper from
responsible sources
FSC® C008047

This book was typeset in Stone Informal and Judy Moody.
The illustrations were created digitally.

Candlewick Press
99 Dover Street
Somerville, Massachusetts 02144

visit us at www.candlewick.com

For my family

M. M.

To Elizabeth Nicholson

P. H. R.

Contents

WISHBONE WISHES

Mary had a lit-tle lamb, lit-tle lamb, lit-tle lamb . . ."

Judy Moody sang as she searched her closet up, down, and sideways. She looked in the dirty clothes pile. P.U.! She looked behind board games. She looked under Mouse the cat. She found her acorn collection, her Popsicle-stick collection, and her wishbone collection.

But no Pilgrim costume.

"Where is it, Mouse?" Judy's cat stuck her paw under the beanbag chair. Judy reached in after her and pulled out an apron string.

Eureka! "Mouse, you're a genius!" There, in all its old-timey black-and-white glory, was her Pilgrim costume. Long dress? *Check.* Apron? *Check.* Pilgrim hat? *Check.* Shoes? Easy-peasy. She could make square buckles out of duct tape and attach them to her sneakers. Under her dress, she would wear her yoga-not-yogurt pants with the go-faster stripes!

Judy could not wait. Only five more days until TTT. Triple T! Turkey-Trot Time. As in Thanksgiving! This year, she, Judy Moody, was going to win the Turkey Trot race. For sure and absolute positive.

Let the countdown begin.

Judy tried her Pilgrim costume on over her clothes to make sure it still fit. She ran downstairs to get the duct tape.

Stink was making a map with . . . kitty litter? "Is that—?" asked Judy. "Never mind. I don't think I want to know."

"It's my desert habitat," said Stink. "You can't tell because it doesn't have any cactuses or Gila monsters yet." He looked up. "Why are you dressed like a Pilgrim?"

"I'm not a Pilgrim," said Judy.

"Then why are you dressed like a girl Paul Revere?"

"You mean Sybil Ludington? I'm not her either."

"Virginia Dare?" Stink asked.

"Guess again." Judy spun around in her dress. "I'm Sarah Josepha Hale." She pronounced each word with importance.

"Sarah Josepha *who*?"

"Sarah Josepha Hale, inventor of Thanksgiving."

"Nah-uh. My teacher said that the Wampanoag people were the inventors of Thanksgiving or something."

"That was the *first* Thanksgiving, Stink. But then everybody forgot about it for like two hundred and forty-some years. It made Sarah Josepha Hale boiling mad. So guess what? She wrote a letter to the president and told him that Thanksgiving should be a holiday. And guess what that Zachary Taylor said?"

"Yes?" wondered Stink.

"N-O. For thirty-eight whole years she wrote letters. Millard Fillmore said no. Franklin Pierce said no. James Buchanan said no."

"Bummer," said Stink. "That's a lot of no."

"Then in 1863, she wrote a letter to President Abraham Lincoln telling him that everybody should eat turkey and give thanks and celebrate Thanksgiving. He listened and agreed to make a Thursday in November a holiday. So, see? Without Sarah Josepha Hale, there would *be* no Thanksgiving."

"Whoa," said Stink. "How come I never heard of her?"

"For your information, she also wrote 'Mary Had a Little Lamb,' Stink."

"You mean 'Mary Had a Little *Turkey*'?" He cracked himself up.

"This Thanksgiving, I'm going to be thankful for Sarah Josepha Hale. What are you thankful for, Stink?"

"I'm thankful your big long story is over," said Stink. He turned back to his kitty-litter map.

"Don't you want to know why I'm dressed like her?" Judy asked.

"Do I have to?" asked Stink.

"It's for Gobblers-a-Go-Go. You know, the festival they have at school on Thanksgiving every year. We always miss it because we're at Grandma Lou's. I begged Mom and Dad to leave for Grandma Lou's *after* the festival. So guess what. This year, we get to *a-go-go*!" Judy cracked herself up.

"Gobblers-a-Go-Go!" Stink said. "Mrs. D. says they have footraces and relay races and a costume parade and a petting zoo and a cakewalk, only it's with pie—"

"Don't forget the Turkey Trot, too. It's a half-mile fun run. We get to wear crazy costumes. Frank is going to be Frankenstein, of course, and Rocky is going to be a blob of slime, and I'm going to be—ta da!—Sarah Josepha Hale."

"I want to run for fun, too. I'll be What's-His-Name, the first astronaut to walk on the moon."

"Neil Armstrong? Why?"

"He ate turkey on the moon. Freeze-dried turkey."

"Weird," said Judy. "But guess what else. The winner wins a for-real Thanksgiving turkey. No lie. I already called Grandma Lou and told her not to buy a turkey this year."

"Not even a backup turkey?" asked Stink. "Just in case you don't win?"

"I'll win. I've been training for weeks. I ran around the block a million times. I ran in place every day on the playground at recess. And I've been eating super-healthy stuff so I'll be in tip-top shape. No sugar. No junk food. And guess what else. I even gave up raisins."

"But you hate raisins—"

"The point is, you have to prepare, Stink," said Judy. "And think positive."

"I'm *positive* that Grandma Lou should get another turkey."

"No way."

"Not even freeze-dried, man-on-the-moon turkey?" Stink asked.

"Not even," said Judy.

"I hope Grandma Lou has lots and lots of cranberries," said Stink. "Or we're going to starve like Pilgrims."

"Hey, I have an idea." Judy ran upstairs and came back with a shoe box.

"Shoes?" asked Stink.

"Wishbones," said Judy. "It's my collection. I've been saving the wishbones from the turkeys at Thanksgiving and sometimes Christmas."

"And we get to make a wish?" asked

Stink. He picked up the biggest V-shaped brown bone of the bunch. "I bet this is a T. rex wishbone. Or I bet it could be a velociraptor furcula."

"A veloci-what-huh?"

"From a dinosaur. Dinosaur wishbone."

"Get real, Stink. A dinosaur wishbone would be as big as a house." Judy grabbed it back. "Anyway, that's my best one. Turkey wishbones only come about once or twice a year. Here, use this one." She handed Stink a pale wishbone.

Stink looked at the measly little bone. "But it's so puny."

"So? It's a chicken wishbone."

"Who ever heard of a chicken wish-bone? You can't wish on a chicken. No way will your wish come true."

"Yes, it will. Let's think of a wish. I know! Let's *both* wish that I win the Turkey Trot. That way I'll be double-sure to win the Thanksgiving turkey."

"But a wish has to be a secret. My wish won't work if you know what it is."

"Fine," said Judy. "Go ahead. Starve like the Pilgrims."

Judy held one end of the wishbone. Stink held the other. They both squeezed their eyes shut, made a wish, and pulled.

Snap!

The wishbone broke in half. Judy

opened her eyes. She held up the bigger
half. "I win!" said Judy, grinning from ear
to ear.

"Lousy chicken wishbone," said Stink.
"I knew my wish wouldn't come true."

"It doesn't matter, Stink. We wished for the same thing. Right?" Stink dug his toe into the rug. "Right?" she asked again. Stink didn't answer.

"Never mind," said Judy. "*I* won the wish, so Turkey Trot, here I come!"

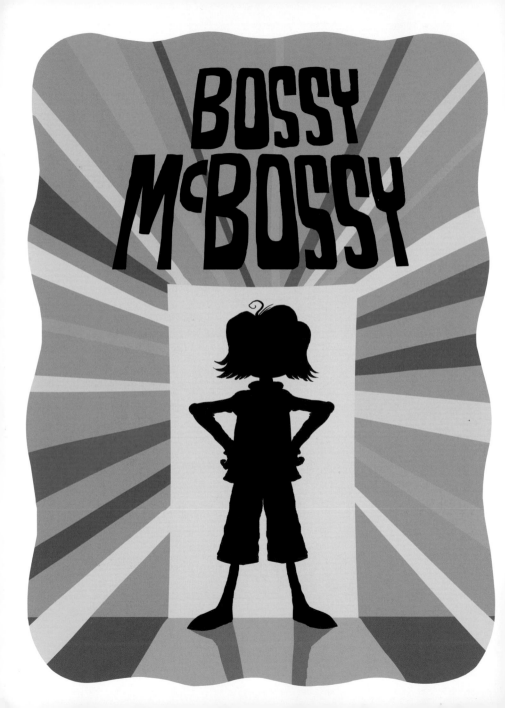

Stink put on his un-smelliest sneakers. He took out his Rapidfire Ultra XE 611M25 stopwatch and started pressing buttons.

Start. Stink hopped on one foot. *Stop.* Ten seconds. *Start.* Stink put a pencil between his toes and wrote *Stink. Stop.* 36.7 seconds. *Start.* Stink stood on one foot and Hula-Hooped in the hallway. *Stop.* 16.3 seconds.

"No Hula-Hooping in the house, Stink," said Judy. "Mom says."

"But I'm practicing skills with my feet. For the footraces at Gobblers-a-Go-Go."

"Footraces just mean you run fast, Stink. Not do other stuff with your feet."

"Well, my feet will be ready for the Turkey Trot."

"Bad news, Stink. You can't be in the Turkey Trot," said Judy.

"Why not?"

"It's for ages eight and up. But you *can* be in the peewee races. The Cranberry Crawl is for babies zero to four, and the Stuffing Strut is for ages five to seven. So you could be in the Cranberry Crawl," Judy teased.

"Hardee-har-har," said Stink. "No fair. What do they have against shrimps?"

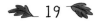 19

"It has nothing to do with being short, Stink. The fun runs have age groups to make it more fair," said Judy. "But you can enter any other contest or race you want. Hey! Want to be my buddy in the Triple Fun Relay?"

"For real?"

"Sure. Why not? It's a relay race with three parts. First is the three-legged race, then the Jell-O race, and last is the human wheelbarrow."

"I like Jell-O," said Stink.

"Yes, but can you balance it on a spoon?"

"Huh?"

"That's the race. You have to cross the

 20

soccer field while holding wriggly-jiggly Jell-O on a spoon, and then pass it to me. Then I have to do it."

"No sweat."

"Okay, then, listen up. We have to get you in shape for the Triple Fun Relay. I'll be your trainer. I've already been practicing like crazy. Give me your stopwatch. I'm going to tell you what to do and I'll time you."

"What is this, the Boss-Stink-Around relay?"

Judy told Stink to hop down the hall. Stink hopped down the hall. *Boing-boing-boing.* Eleven seconds. "Faster!" said Judy. He hopped over to the stairs. Nine seconds.

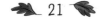

"Faster, Stink!" Stink hopped back to his room. Seventeen seconds.

He plopped down on the floor, out of breath. "So. Much. Hopping," said Stink. "I feel like a bunny."

"Aw. Poor bunny," said Judy. "You'll thank me when we win the three-legged race." She handed Stink a Nancy Drew book. "Now walk across the room balancing this on your head, and I'll time you."

"Why?"

"It helps with balance, Stink. Trust me. This will prepare you for the Jell-O part of the relay. Ready?"

"Ready, Freddy."

Stink put the book on his head and

started to walk. Halfway across the room, the book went sliding off of his head and crashed to the ground.

"Don't you have a book that's not so slippery?" Stink asked.

"I don't have any bumpy books, Stink. C'mon. Try again."

He crossed the room with the book on

his head. Seven seconds. He crossed the room again. Five seconds. He did it again. Six seconds.

"Good!" said Judy. "Now let me see you *crawl* up the stairs this time."

"Crawl? What for? The Cranberry Crawl is for babies."

Judy made a muscle with her arm. "Muscles, Stink-o. You have to have strong arm muscles to be a human wheelbarrow."

"Okay, Bossy McBossy."

Stink crawled up the stairs on all fours. Twenty-one seconds. Stink crawled down the stairs. Seventeen seconds. Stink crawled up the stairs. Nineteen seconds. Stink crawled down the stairs.

"That's it," said Stink, plopping down on the bottom step. "I demand Jell-O."

"Hel-lo! Sugar!" Judy reached into her back pocket. "Here, you can have an energy bar instead."

"Energy bars taste like cardboard!" said Stink.

"Get used to it, Stink. No sugar until after the race. And no junk food. And nothing that ends in -ose."

"Mmm. Now I want tacos. Or nachos. Or mangoes."

"I mean no glucose, fructose, sucrose, et cetera. Those are all just fancy-dancy words for sugar."

"But Jell-O is fruit. And it ends in *O*, not -*ose*. Jell-O is way cool. Did you know that the way it jiggles mimics brain waves? And it has a super hush-hush secret code on every box that I bet only the president of Jell-O knows? And it's the official state snack food of Utah. No lie."

"Then I guess you'll have to move to Utah."

"Not even one teeny-weeny cranberry Jiggler? C'mon. They only have that flavor once a year."

"Not even," said Judy. "Tell you what. We can practice with tofu on a spoon. We'll race down the hall and back."

"Tofu is gross," Stink said.

"Well, we're *not* going to eat it," said Judy.

"I'm pooped," said Stink. "How about if I time *you* for a while?"

"No chance, Lance."

"Then give me back my stopwatch," said Stink.

"No way, McNay."

"But it's *my* Rapidfire Ultra stopwatch!"

"You're ultra cuckoo if you think I'm

giving this back. We need it to get ready for the Triple Fun Relay, and you said you'd do whatever I say."

"That was before you turned into Bosszilla!" said Stink.

"Did not!" Judy said.

"Did too!"

"Not!" said Judy.

Judy held the stopwatch in the air, high over Stink's head. Stink jumped up and tried to grab it. "Gimme!"

If only Stink were taller. He got up on a footstool. He tried to jump, but the stool tipped over and Stink landed on the floor with a crash. He knocked a framed photo off the table and the glass broke.

"Uh-oh," said Judy.

"Kids!" said Mom, coming into the room. "What in the world's going on in here?"

"Judy thinks she's the boss of me *and* she won't let me have Jell-O *and* she won't give me back my stopwatch."

"Stink said I could use it. We're getting ready for the Triple Fun Relay," said Judy.

"Okay, both of you need a time-out. Go to your rooms. And I want you to stay there for one hour," Mom told them in her I-am-not-kidding voice.

Judy stared at the floor. Stink stared at the stopwatch in Judy's hand.

"Stink, let's see how fast you can get to your room," said Judy. "I'll time you."

Yoink! Stink snatched the stopwatch

out of Judy's hand. He raced up the stairs and down the hall and into his room and slammed the door.

Slam! Judy slammed her door back. Her *Stink-Free Zone* doorknob doohickey fell to the floor.

4:35 p.m. Judy's room

Judy looked around her room. One hour! What was she going to do stuck in her room for one whole hour? They should call this *time-in,* not *time-out.*

Judy practiced running in place in her not-Pilgrim costume. As she ran, she thought about Stink, WMAB. World's Most Annoying Brother. Why was he always bugging her? Look what he did. He went and got her into big trouble.

4:37 p.m. Stink's room

Stink looked around his room. One hour! What was he going to do stuck in his room for one whole hour? He might as well be in not-Monopoly jail. Do not pass GO. Do not collect two hundred dollars. *They should call this* time-in, *not* time-out, Stink thought.

If only Judy, aka Bossy McBossy, had not gotten him into big trouble. He could be eating Jell-O (with tacos, nachos, or mangoes) right now.

4:39 p.m. Judy's room

Judy played checkers with Mouse. Judy speed-read a whole chapter of Nancy Drew to Mouse. Mouse curled up in her lap while Judy finger-knitted two inches onto her giant yarn chain.

4:46 p.m. Stink's room

Stink snapped the last of 253 pieces in place on his motorcycle made of Snappos. Stink fed Toady. Stink played Hide-the-Undies with Astro. Stink made Charlie the dummy talk without moving his lips. But nobody was there to hear.

4:52 p.m. Judy's room

There was nothing left to do but home-work. On a Saturday. At least it was fun homework. Judy took out the shoe box from under her desk. She, Judy Moody, was making a Thanksgiving diorama for

Social Studies. It was due Monday. Her teacher, Mr. Todd, was going to put all the dioramas on display at Gobblers-a-Go-Go!

Judy's diorama did not have a turkey. It did not have a Pilgrim. It did not have a pumpkin or a squash. It had miniature acorn people!

Judy drew a face on an acorn. The acorn people were Abraham Lincoln and yours truly, Sarah Josepha Hale. She made a teeny-tiny acorn-hat for Sarah J. and a teeny-tiny stovepipe hat for Abe.

While the glue dried, Judy made a teeny-tiny 1863 calendar and circled the last Thursday in November.

She wrote a teeny-tiny letter, just like the one that Sarah Josepha Hale sent to Abe Lincoln. A letter asking him to make Thanksgiving a national holiday. And guess what—Abe Lincoln said Y-E-S yes!

Eureka! Mr. Todd was going to flip when he saw this. A giant red A-plus-plus danced before Judy's eyes.

4:57 p.m. Stink's room

There was nothing left to do but homework. Stink got out his worksheet from Mrs. D.

List ten facts about turkeys.

1. Wild turkeys sleep in trees.
2. Judy is a turkey.

3. One turkey has about 5,000 feathers.

4. Judy is a turkey.

5. A wild turkey's call sounds like "turk-turk-turk."

6. The ugly thing that grows over a turkey's bill is a snood.

7. The ugly thing that hangs from the turkey's neck is called a wattle.

8. Judy is a snood.

9. Judy is a wattle.

10. Judy is a turkey-lurkey.

5:12 p.m. Judy's room

Judy opened her door a crack, trying not to make a sound. She did not want Super-Spy Stink to catch her. If she got caught, she'd have to do more time-out.

 39

She stuck her head out the door. She looked up and down the hall. The coast was crystal clear! She tiptoed past Stink's room. She tiptoed into Mom and Dad's room. She picked up the phone to call Grandma Lou.

5:13 p.m. Stink's room

Stink thought he heard something in the hall. He opened his door just a crack, trying not to make a sound. He looked up and down the hall. Nobody and nothing. Not even Mouse.

Stink tilted his head to listen. *Pssh. Pssh.* He heard Judy whispering on the phone! What a rat. What a fink. What a rat fink. Who gave her a Get-Out-of-Jail-Free card?

Stink crept to the doorway of Mom and Dad's room. He listened. He heard the word *turkey* a bunch of times. Was Judy calling Grandma Lou? Was Judy telling Grandma Lou not to buy a turkey for Thanksgiving?

5:13:11 p.m. Mom and Dad's room

"Hello? Grandma Lou, it's Judy," whispered Judy.

"Hi, Pickle," said Grandma Lou. "Why are you whispering?"

"Long story," whispered Judy. "I just called to ask, Did you buy a turkey yet?"

"Not yet," said Grandma Lou.

"Good," said Judy. "Because don't forget, I'm going to Gobblers-a-Go-Go this year. It's a festival at my school, and I'm going to be getting a turkey there."

"Hmm. I remember. Maybe I should get a backup turkey. You know, just in case."

"No backup turkeys!" said Judy. "Do you double-promise pinkie-swear?"

"I promise," said Grandma Lou.

"Good!" said Judy.

"See you Thursday!" said Grandma Lou.

"And Friday and Saturday and Sunday," said Judy. "Dad says we get to stay the whole weekend!"

5:13:37 p.m. Mom and Dad's room

Stink crawled into the room on all fours. Judy had her back to him. He slid on his belly across the carpet. He slid under the bed. He waited until Judy hung up the phone. Stink Moody, Super-Spy Guy, did not dare to breathe.

5:14 p.m. Mom and Dad's room

Judy heard Stink slither into the room. What a snake! She saw his stinky sneaker sticking out from under the bed. What a Sneaky McSneaker. What a Stinky McStinker. Did he really think that she didn't know he was spying on her from under the bed? She, Judy Moody, Girl Detective, would out-sneak Stink. She would out-Stink him, too.

5:15 p.m. Mom and Dad's room

As soon as the coast was clear, Stink crawled out from under the bed. He oh-so-quietly picked up the phone. He hit REDIAL. *Dee-dee-dee-dee-da-da-da.* The phone dialed. Stink heard Grandma Lou's voice. It was her answering machine.

Stink left a message. "Grandma Lou, this is Stink. Please get a backup turkey. I repeat. Emergency. Backup turkey needed for Thanksgiving, over and out."

He sure hoped Grandma Lou got the message.

5:17 p.m. Stink's room

Judy slipped into Stink's room. She searched around for the stopwatch. *Snatcheroo!* She grabbed it and ran.

5:18 p.m. Stink's room

Stink patted himself on the back for being

a super-sneaky spy guy. He tiptoed back to his room. He went to check his stopwatch. Wait just a sixty-second minute! His stopwatch was nowhere in sight.

Rat-fink sister strikes again!

He looked at the clock. Eighteen and a half more time-out minutes to go.

5:18 p.m. Judy's room

Eighteen and a half more minutes to go. One hour of time-out felt like three hours of regular time. No, more like three days.

If only Stink were not such a stinky little brother. They would not have gotten into a fight. They would not be in time-out for what felt like three years.

Judy held the stopwatch. Judy clicked

the stopwatch. Judy timed herself finger-knitting one inch. Forty-six seconds.

Timing things wasn't as much fun without Stink. Judy stopped the stopwatch. *Stink's* stopwatch. The thing that had started the fight to begin with. The fight that Stink started! It was all his fault that the picture got broken and landed them in a time-out!

Judy twisted her mood ring. Well, maybe not *all* his fault. It *was* Stink's stopwatch. And she *had* been hogging it. She hated to admit it, but Stink was right about her being Bossy McBossy.

Judy had an idea. A peace-treaty idea. Just like the Pilgrims and the Wampanoags. She would draw up a

peace treaty between herself and Stink.
She hoped he would sign it.

PEACE TREATY BETWEEN JUDY AND STINK E. MOODY

In order to secure perpetual peace and harmony (aka no fighting) between Party of the First (Judy) and Party of the Second (Stink), these articles are set forth as the new Moody rule and law on this twenty-first day of November.

Article 1: Party of the First (Judy) will SURRENDER THE STOPWATCH and return it to rightful owner (Stink).

Article 2: Party of the First (Judy) SWEARS ON NANCY DREW not to be Bossy McBossy for a period of time no less than three days and no greater than five days.

Article 3: Party of the First (Judy) will ALLOW Party of the Second (Stink) TO EAT JELL-O as soon as the Triple Fun Relay is over.

Article 4: Party of the Second (Stink) promises NOT TO BE ANNOYING for period of time set forth in Article 2 above.

If both parties agree, they will sign in cursive, using quill pen if possible:

_____   _____
JUDY MOODY   STINK E. MOODY

To further seal the deal, each party must kiss the feet of Toady. If either party breaks the peace treaty, they will be forced to eat stinky sushi.

5:25 p.m. Judy's room

Judy tiptoed across the hall and slipped the peace treaty under Stink's door. She tiptoed back to her room.

5:26 p.m. Stink's room

Stink saw a piece of paper fly under his door. A peace treaty! Cool-o!

He read the treaty. He was all for peace. He was all for getting his stopwatch back. He was all for Jell-O.

He signed the treaty in his best cursive. He ran across the hall and slipped it under Judy's door.

5:31 p.m. Judy's room

Judy's door opened a crack. Out came

a hand. The hand was holding a stopwatch. Stink's stopwatch! Stink grabbed it and ran back to his room. He stood in the doorway with the door open. *Beep! Beep! Beep!* He pressed a bunch of buttons on his Rapidfire Ultra XE 611M25.

5:32 p.m. Hallway

Judy opened her door all the way. She stood in the doorway. Across the hall, Stink stood in the doorway to his room.

"I'm sorry I was Bossy McBossy," said Judy.

"I'm sorry I called you a turkey," said Stink. "And a snood. And a wattle."

"When?"

"Oh! Never mind."

"So. We have a peace treaty, right?" Judy asked. She held out her hand. "Want to shake hands or something?"

"We still have three more minutes of time-out," said Stink. "So technically, I can't come out of my room yet."

"Oh. Right. Me either."

Judy and Stink stayed in their doorways. They did not cross the thresholds. They did not set a foot in the hallway. Not even one toe.

"How many more minutes, Stink?" Judy asked.

"Two more minutes . . . and twenty-three seconds," said Stink, looking at his stopwatch.

Judy and Stink waited some more.

"How many more minutes now?"

"One minute, sixteen seconds."

Stink started counting down. "Five, four, three, two, one!" Lights flashed and the Rapidfire Ultra beeped like crazy. "Woo-hoo! Jail time is over!"

Stink set his stopwatch to zero and clicked START again. Judy and Stink celebrated fifty-one whole minutes of peace until it was time for dinner.

FLYING TURKEY GIZZARDS

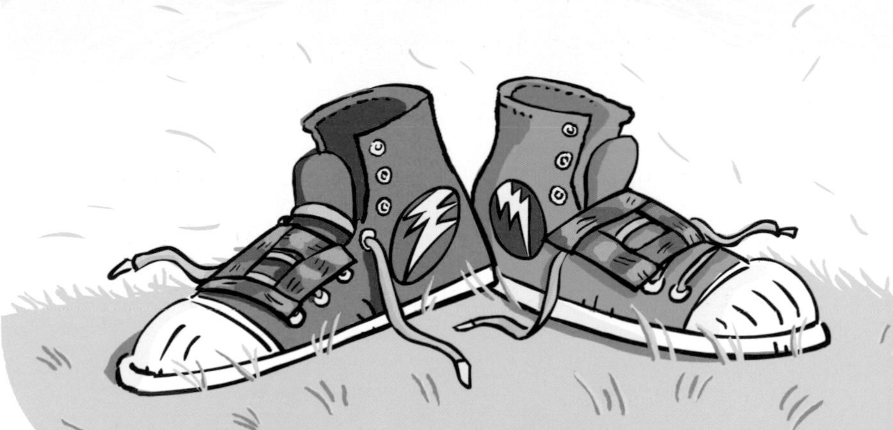

The next day was Peace Treaty Day. Judy and Stink did not get in a fight all day Sunday. Or Monday. Or Tuesday. Or Wednesday. Four whole days! Not even when Stink stuck his smelly sneakers under Judy's nose. Not even when Judy bossed Stink to keep him from eating gummy-shark candy. Not even!

For four whole days, they jumped rope, crawled up and ran down stairs, and practiced relays with tofu on a spoon. They did not eat candy or drink soda. They stayed away from junk food and anything that ended in *-ose.* They munched on carrot sticks and drank water and got plenty of sleep.

At last it was Thursday. Thanksgiving. Turkey-Trot Time!

Stink got out his stopwatch and started timing Judy just for fun. He timed Judy brushing her teeth. Forty-two seconds. He timed Judy brushing her hair. Zero seconds. He timed Judy putting on her Pilgrim costume. Sixty-six seconds. He timed her sneeze at .8 seconds.

He timed Judy eating her peanut-butter no-jelly brown-bread toast. Three minutes to fix it. Sixty-one seconds to eat it, not counting three gulps of coconut water in between.

"Stink, I'm going to amend the peace treaty if you don't stop timing everything I do!"

"Time to go!" called Mom. Judy grabbed her Pilgrim hat, her wishbone collection, and her Mood Libs to take to Grandma Lou's. She stuck one of the wishbones in her apron pocket for good luck. Stink grabbed his moon boots, his travel Trouble game, and his motorcycle made of 253 Snappos. Dad grabbed a bag of canned food for the food drive.

@ @ @

When they got to Virginia Dare School, the Gobblers-a-Go-Go festivities were already under way. Kids and families crowded the school grounds. Signs said TURKEY BOWLING, CAKEWALK, PETTING ZOO. Live turkeys strutted around inside a pen, and kids learned to turkey call. A band called the Snoods and Wattles plucked banjos in the background.

On the way to the parade, Judy and Stink found the table with all the dioramas made by the third-graders in Mr. Todd's class.

"Stink, I can't look. Did I get an A-plus-plus?" Judy asked.

"Better," said Stink. "You got a way-cool sticker!"

Judy stared at the sticker with

vegetables on it. "I got a *corn* sticker? So my diorama is corny?"

"Not just corn," said Stink. "The Three Sisters: corn, beans, and squash. It's on the back of my gold dollar. The one with Sacagawea. Only, in the old days, corn was called maize."

Judy beamed. "So my diorama is a-*maize*-ing!" Stink cracked up.

Judy and Stink ran to join the costume parade. She waved to Frankenstein (aka Frank) and a slime blob (aka Rocky), who were already lined up. Frank was wearing a sign that said HAPPY FRANKSGIVING!

"That's funny!" Judy told her friend.

Rocky had a string tied around his

neck. "What's with the string?" Judy asked.

"I'm a balloon slime!" said Rocky. "Like in the Thanksgiving Day parade in New York City."

"Wow," said Judy. "Great idea."

"I'm a balloon, too," said Stink.

"Na-uh. You're an astronaut," said Judy.

"Astronaut *balloon*," said Stink.

"Where's your string?" Rocky asked.

"Um, see, I'm the balloon that broke free and floated over the parade." Stink held out his arms and pretended to fly.

"So you're a Pilgrim again, huh?" Rocky said to Judy.

"She's a three-names lady, the Inventor

of Thanksgiving and 'Mary Had a Little Lamb,'" Stink piped in before Judy could answer. Judy rolled her eyes.

"Sarah Josepha Hale," said Judy.

"Run," said Stink, "before she gives you a history lesson."

"I'm entering three events today," said Judy. "If I win the best costume contest, the Triple Fun Relay, *and* the Turkey Trot, I'll end up with a Thanksgiving center-piece, a pumpkin pie for dessert, and a turkey to take to Grandma Lou's."

"Hey, it's time!" said Stink.

All the kids in costume lined up and marched in a parade to the tune of "What a Wonderful World." They paraded past the panel of judges.

In no time, Ms. Tuxedo, the principal, stepped up to the podium to announce a winner. A hush fell over the crowd. "The prize for best costume this year is a cornucopia." She held up a horn-shaped basket full of grapes and oranges and stalks of corn. "It will make a beautiful centerpiece for your holiday table. And the winner for best costume is . . . Jessica A. Finch."

"Where is she?" asked Frank.

"*What* is she?" asked Judy.

An ear of corn waddled up onstage. The ear of corn was Jessica Finch. And she was holding a leash. At the end of the leash was her pet potbellied pig.

"Hey," said Frank. "There's that pig she got for her birthday."

"PeeGee WeeGee," said Judy. "I pig-sat him."

PeeGee WeeGee was dressed as a Pilgrim! Jessica Finch accepted her prize. She tried to take a bow, but her corn costume wouldn't bend. *Pop! Pop-pop-pop!* Kernels of corn popped off of her costume as she tried to lean over.

"I can't believe we got beat by corn on the cob," said Judy.

"I can't believe we got beat by pop-corn," said Frank.

"They just picked her because her pet pig is cute," said Stink.

"PeeGee *is* a pretty cute Pilgrim," Judy admitted. "But Frank's costume is so funny. And Rocky's is creative. Nobody else came as a parade balloon."

"Except me," Stink piped in.

"And yours is hysterical *and* historical," Frank told Judy.

"Thanks," said Judy. "I had to sleep in curlers to get these corkscrew curls to come out right." *Boing!* She bounced a curl. "I'll bet those judges didn't even know I was

66

Sarah Josepha Hale. I'll bet they thought I was just a plain-old, boring-old Pilgrim."

"You should have won the corny horn," said Stink.

"There's still the Triple Fun Relay," said Judy. "And don't forget the Turkey Trot. But the Flying Giblets are going to win the relay race hands down."

"Who are the Flying Giblets?" asked Stink.

"Us," said Judy. "You and me."

"Aren't giblets all the yucky parts of the turkey?" asked Stink.

"Yep," said Frank. "Livers and kidneys and gizzards. Yuck! My dog, Sparky, loves them."

"Gross," said Judy.

"Sweet," said Stink. "We're the Flying Turkey Gizzards!"

@ @ @

Relay-race time! The Flying Turkey Gizzards lined up at the starting line next to FrankenSlime (aka Frank and Rocky) and tons of other kids paired up in teams like Scrambled Legs, Phoebe and Jay, and Captain Runderpants.

"Listen up, Stink," Judy said, hiking up her skirt to duct-tape her left ankle to Stink's right ankle. "First we do the three-legged race across the soccer field to those orange cones. Then I'll go first with the Jell-O. You run back to the other side, and I'll pass it off to you. Then we zoom

through the human-wheelbarrow race, and that pumpkin pie is ours."

"Got it," said Stink.

Mr. Todd was in charge of the Triple Fun Relay. "On your mark, get set, GO!" he called. Judy and Stink hopped across the field.

"Flying Turkey Gizzards rule!" she called to Rocky and Frank.

They were ahead. So far, so good. When they reached the orange cones, Stink yanked off the tape and ran back to the starting line while Judy grabbed a spoon with two cubes of red Jell-O on it. She started across the field. It wiggled. It jiggled. It made Judy giggle.

In no time, she passed the spoon to Stink. He headed across the field, holding the spoon out in front of him. *Yum, yum,* he thought. *Two bright-red cubes of wiggling, jiggling Jell-O. Once-a-year cranberry Jell-O . . . with pretzels . . . my favorite!*

Stink could not stop staring at the spoon. He forgot to look up. He forgot to look down. All of a sudden, one of those wiggly, jiggly Jell-O cubes slid right off of the spoon. It fell—*plop*—onto the ground. Stink stood and stared.

"Stink!" Judy yelled. "Go! Never, ever stop!" He rushed to the finish line.

Human-wheelbarrow time!

Stink crouched on the ground, and Judy grabbed his ankles. She started to steer him back across the field. "Don't worry, Stink. This is our best event. This is where the Flying Turkey Gizzards make up time and bring home the pie."

They were halfway across the field when Stink suddenly stopped. He saw something in the grass. Something wiggly. Something jiggly. It was not a worm. It was Jell-O. Oh-so-mouth-watering cranberry-pretzel Jell-O.

He did not bother to make sure it was dirt-free. He did not bother to make sure it was ant-free. He grabbed the Jell-O and—*glup!*—stuck it in his mouth.

All of a sudden, Judy could not steer Stink. She pushed his legs, but they did not move one inch. She tripped over Stink and fell flat on her face.

Stink sat up. He had a red face—a face full of Jell-O. All the other teams had made it to the finish line. The Flying Turkey Gizzards were finished. As in over and done with. As in defeated, destroyed, did-not-win.

"We have a winner!" called Mr. Todd. Frank and Rocky, aka FrankenSlime, held their hands in the air like champs.

"Way to go, guys," said Judy.

Stink licked his lips. "Sorry we didn't win," he mumbled.

"I hope you liked your Jell-O," said Judy, "because we're sure not getting any pie."

Turkey-Trot Time! Judy trotted over to the track with Rocky and Frank. Stink tried to follow them.

"Stink, the peewee races are over on the playground," Judy teased. "Go strut your stuffing."

Stink stood on his tiptoes. "I'm tall enough to pass for eight years old."

Judy snorted. "You're barely tall enough to pass for *five* years old. Bye, Stink." Judy waved as Stink headed off for the peewee races.

This was it. The big kahuna. Turkey-palooza. The moment Judy had been waiting for. For three whole weeks she had been getting ready for this race!

Judy thought of all the times she had eaten an energy bar (seventeen). She thought of all the times she had run around the block (seventy-three) and jumped rope (seven hundred). She thought of all the times she did not eat sugar (seven gazillion).

Okay, so maybe there would be no corn-horn thingy for Grandma Lou's Thanksgiving table. Maybe there would be no pumpkin pie for dessert. But what was Thanksgiving without turkey?

She, Judy Moody, just had to win the Turkey Trot.

Judy pushed down on her Pilgrim hat. She tightened the laces on her lucky high-tops (one green, one orange). She straightened her go-faster stripes.

Reaching into her apron pocket, Judy rubbed her wishbone for extra good luck.

Judy lined up at the start, next to Frankenstein and Slime. There were turkeys and hockey players, Pilgrims and pirates and princesses. There were two brides and one Chewbacca. There was even one tall kid dressed as a pie crust.

She pointed her toe at the finish line, just itch-itch-itching to run. Excitement prickled down her arms and tickled the back of her neck. Judy looked down at her sneakers and imagined they had wings.

At last, Mr. Todd raised his hand in the air. "On your mark, get set, go!"

They were off! Judy stayed neck and neck with FrankenSlime on the first half of the first lap. Chewbacca and a couple of turkeys got ahead of her. She told herself it was okay to get a little behind. She told herself to save her energy for the last lap.

Halfway around the track, Judy tried to think of fast things. Race cars. Roller coasters. Roadrunners. She imagined she was a bolt of lightning. She imagined she was Mercury, with wings on his feet. She imagined she was Supergirl, faster than the speed of light.

On the second lap around the track, she had her get-up-and-go-go working. She did not see Mom and Dad waving from the crowd. She did not see Jessica Finch making funny faces. She did not hear Mr. Todd cheering his third-graders on.

She was flying! She, Judy Moody, was a mean, green-and-orange-footed flying machine.

There was no stopping her now. She was out in front of Rocky and Frank. She left two pirates, one princess, and one hockey player in the dust. And she had almost caught up with Chewbacca.

Then, out of nowhere, just as Judy was rounding the bend, something ran out onto the track. Something pink, something plump. Something porcine in a Pilgrim costume. Something *pig*.

Mary Had a Little Piggy! It was PeeGee WeeGee. He had run right smack-dab out into the middle of the race. That little piggy went *wee, wee, wee, wee* all the way down the track.

All of a sudden, PeeGee stopped. A pirate tripped over that pig. A princess flipped over that pig. PeeGee sniffed the air. PeeGee tore off after Judy.

OINK!

The crowd was yelling now. "Look out!"

"Pig on the loose!"

"Catch that pig!"

PeeGee zigged and zagged across the track. That squealing ball of pig cut right in front of Judy. She zoomed after him. "PeeGee! Come back here, you little oinker!" *Sarah J. Hale to the rescue!*

PeeGee ran pig-fast. PeeGee ran figure eights around Judy. He knocked over one, two, three orange traffic cones.

Judy burned rubber. She chased after that pig like it was a greased-pig-chasing contest. She chased after that pig like greased lightning. Her Pilgrim hat flew off. Her hair came out of its Sarah J. Hale sausage-roll curls. The shoe buckles took wing — right off of her sneakers.

But Judy kept on running. She ran right past Pie Crust and left Chewy in the dust.

PeeGee crossed the finish line. Judy was right at his heels. She reached out and quick-as-a-thief grabbed that little piggy.

The crowd went hog wild. They chanted "PeeGee! PeeGee!" Then Judy heard another chant.

"Ju-dy! Ju-dy!" She broke out into a grin. PeeGee may have crossed the finish line first, but she, Judy Moody, was the human-being winner of the Turkey Trot! For real and absolute positive!

Jessica Finch came running up to Judy.

"Sorry about PeeGee," she said. "When he saw you run past, he squirmed right out of my arms."

"Are you kidding?" said Judy, handing over PeeGee. "He saved my bacon. I might not have won the Turkey Trot without him." She glanced around. "Want to know a secret? I wished on a wishbone that I'd win the race, and this little piggy helped my wish come true. Pig's honor!" Wait till she told Stink that the puny chicken wishbone had worked after all.

"Sweet," said Jessica, scratching Pee-Gee behind his ears.

"*And* I promised my Grandma Lou I'd bring the turkey." Judy rubbed noses with

PeeGee. "So you *could* say this guy helped me save Thanksgiving."

Just then, Stink came running up to Judy. "I won! I won, I won, I won!"

Judy couldn't help laughing. "What did you win, Stink?"

"My race. The Stuffing Strut."

"What *prize* did you win?" Judy asked.

"Nothing."

"C'mon, Stink. You must have won something."

"Okay, but don't laugh." He held up a bag. A plastic bag full of boring-old hard, stale bread cubes.

"Stuffing!" Judy said, trying to sound excited. "That's great!"

Stink peered at the bag again. "It is?"

"I know it looks crummy, Stink—"

"It *is* crummy. It's *crumbs*. Stale old bread crumbs."

"But Grandma Lou will make it into yummy-not-crummy stuffing, I promise. C'mon, Stink. Let's go get the big kahuna. The Turkeypalooza."

"Huh?"

"My prize for winning the Turkey Trot. The Thanksgiving turkey. Here comes Mr. Todd now." Rocky and Frank held one end of a cooler, and Mr. Todd was holding the other. They plunked the cooler on the ground. Mr. Todd lifted the lid. Judy and Stink leaned over and peered at . . . a fifteen-pound freaky frozen hunk of . . . football?

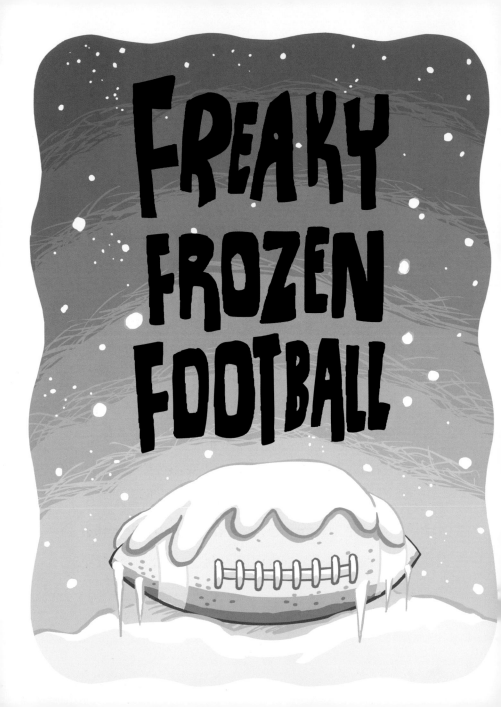

Something was wrong. Way wrong. This was *not* what she, Judy Moody, had wished for. A freaky frozen football wrapped in plastic was no-way, no-how, *not* her wishbone wish!

"Is it a frozen football?" Judy asked Mr. Todd.

"It's Frosty the Snow Turkey!" Stink said.

"I know it doesn't exactly look like Tom Terrific," said Mr. Todd, "but it's still a turkey."

"Turkeys are brown and juicy," said Judy, "not pale and goose-bumpy."

"And they smell good," said Stink. "And they have gravy."

"This bird just isn't cooked yet," said Mr. Todd. "It'll be brown and juicy and smell good once it's roasted. You'll see."

"What about the gravy?" asked Stink.

"C'mon, Stink. Grandma Lou will know what to do," said Judy, lugging the cooler to the car with Stink.

Judy and Stink said their thank-yous. Judy and Stink said their good-byes. "Happy Franksgiving!" Judy called to her friends.

Judy scooped up her a-maize-ing diorama from the display table. Soon the

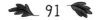

Moodys were loaded into the car, turkey and all. At last, Judy and Stink were on their way to Grandma Lou's house. Thanksgiving, here we come!

֎ ֎ ֎

"Over the river and through the woods, to Grandma Lou's we go. . . ."

Judy and Stink were in a silly Happy-Thanksgiving-y mood. They sat in the backseat, singing at the top of their lungs, the cooler of turkey between them.

Judy looked at the cooler. "I can almost smell that turkey," she said. "Crispy on the outside. Juicy on the inside."

"Ahh, the smell of Thanksgiving," said Stink.

They played car games to take their

minds off of turkey. Soon Stink felt carsick. They stopped to get fresh air. They stopped when the bridge opened. They stopped for Dad to get coffee. They stopped for Mom to gaze at a blue heron.

Stink stuck his head up into the front seat. "Are we there yet?" he asked. *Cr-runch!* He stepped on a shoe box.

"Hey!" Judy cried. "That's my diorama." She yanked the box out from under Stink's feet. "Mom! Dad! Bigfoot here just wrecked my diorama! I brought it for Grandma Lou to use as a Thanksgiving centerpiece."

She turned to Stink. "For a short person, you sure have big feet." Stink made a face. Judy made a face back. "Hand over my wishbone collection, too, before you wreck that."

Stink pointed to his Snappos motorcycle in the pocket of the door on Judy's side. "Then give me my motorcycle. I brought it to show Grandma Lou."

"Judy. Stink. What happened to that peace treaty of yours?" Mom asked.

"No fighting on Thanksgiving, kids," said Dad. "We're almost there."

"You said that a half hour ago," said Stink. But they had already passed Mt. Trashmore. Just then, Stink saw the giant gorilla in a Hawaiian shirt at the entrance to Ocean Breeze.

"Hugh Mongous!" Judy and Stink

called out at the same time. That meant they were almost there.

They cracked up. "Jinx. You owe me . . . Jell-O," said Stink.

"You owe me one not-smushed Thanksgiving centerpiece," said Judy.

"We're here!" Dad called, pulling into the driveway.

Judy and Stink bounded out of the car. Pugsy, Grandma Lou's pug, ran out to meet them. He jumped on them. He licked Judy and Stink up and down and all over. Grandma Lou gave everybody Happy-Thanksgiving hugs.

Mom and Dad carried the cooler into the kitchen. Everyone, including Pugsy, piled in after them.

Stink sniffed the air. "Mmm. I can already smell that turkey!" said Stink.

"Yes, let's see that turkey of yours, Judy," said Grandma Lou.

Judy flipped up the latch on the cooler. She flipped up the second latch. Carefully, she lifted the lid. "*Ta da!* Presenting . . . Tom Terrific!"

"Uh-oh," said Mom and Dad.

"Uh-oh," said Grandma Lou.

"What-oh?" asked Judy.

Grandma Lou wrinkled her forehead. She *umm*ed and *hmm*ed a lot. She poked the turkey a few times with her finger.

Dad lifted the bird so they could peek underneath.

"This could take hours to thaw," said Grandma Lou.

"Oh, no," Judy groaned.

"Plus . . . at least four more hours to roast."

"Nuh-uh," Stink moaned.

"That would put Thanksgiving dinner at about midnight!"

"Rare!" said Judy.

"Cool!" said Stink.

"That's too late," said Mom. "We don't want Grandma Lou up cooking till the middle of the night."

"We'd all be in a *fowl* mood by then," said Dad. Everybody cracked up.

"The turkey at the White House got a presidential pardon! We'll just have to give Tom Terrific a pardon, too," said Stink.

"I think it's a little late for Tom Terrific here," said Dad.

"Sorry, Grandma Lou," Judy said. "I practiced really hard so I could win the turkey and—"

"She did!" said Stink. "She jumped rope and gave up sugar and junk food and everything."

"I just didn't think it would be *frozen*."

"Worse than Antarctica!" said Stink.

"And I made you promise not to get a backup turkey and everything."

"But *I* asked Grandma Lou to get a backup turkey, just in case," said Stink. He turned to Grandma Lou. "You *did* get a backup turkey, right?"

Grandma Lou shook her head no.

"Sorry I ruined Thanksgiving," Judy said.

Grandma Lou put her arm around Judy. "You didn't ruin Thanksgiving, Pickle. The important thing is that we're all together."

Dad wrestled the turkey into the fridge.

"Besides," said Grandma Lou, "this turkey will be defrosted by tomorrow. We can roast it and eat it then. It'll be like having two Thanksgivings."

"Wow! Two Thanksgivings!" said Stink. "Instead of leftovers tomorrow, we'll have *first*overs."

"But what about today?" Judy asked.

Stink ran over to his backpack and pulled out the bag of bread crumbs. "We have stuffing!" said Stink. "I won it in the Stuffing Strut."

"Perfect," said Grandma Lou. "And I have mashed potatoes and green beans and cranberry sauce. Now all we need is a main dish."

"Peanut butter and jelly?" asked Stink.

"Tuna fish?" asked Mom.

"Grandma Lou's famous spaghetti pie?" asked Dad.

Judy frowned. "But it's just not Thanksgiving without *turkey.*"

Grandma Lou wagged a finger at Judy. "You just gave me an idea. Maybe we can save Thanksgiving after all."

Grandma Lou rushed over to the fridge.
She searched the top shelf. She searched
the bottom shelf. She searched behind
tubs of yogurt and jars of pickles.

"*Ta da!*" said Grandma Lou. She held
up a package of . . .

"Hot dogs?" said Judy.

"Hot dogs?" said Stink.

"Not just any old hot dogs," said
Grandma Lou. "*Turkey* hot dogs!"

"Turkey?" said Judy.

"Turkey?" said Stink.

"Turkey franks!" said Grandma Lou. "We can grill them up, slap them on a bun, add a little stuffing and cranberry sauce for Thanksgiving flair. What do you think?"

"Genius!" said Judy, nodding.

"And guess what," said Stink. "They didn't even eat turkey at the first Thanksgiving."

"Really?" said Grandma Lou. "Then what did they have?"

"Corn. And beans and squash."

"I have beans. But I don't have any corn *or* squash," said Grandma Lou.

"Not even a *corn*ucopia?" asked Judy.

"We could make popcorn," said Stink. "Popcorn is corn."

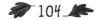

Judy dashed to the front room and came back with her diorama. "And I brought a *squashed* centerpiece," said Judy. "This could be our squash!"

The whole family laughed their heads off.

Judy turned the shoe box to show Grandma Lou. "This is a diorama of the moment when Sarah Josepha Hale—"

"Invented Thanksgiving!" said Stink.

Judy pointed to the acorn people. "See? This is Sarah J. and this is Abraham Lincoln. She sent him a letter saying that Thanksgiving should be a holiday."

"Creative," said Grandma Lou. "Let's put this on the table. Very inspiring centerpiece, Judy!"

Judy beamed. Stink ran and got his motorcycle made of 253 Snappos. He added it to the centerpiece. "Stink," said Judy, "I don't think they had motorcycles at the first Thanksgiving."

Dad grilled the turkey dogs. Grandma

Lou made stuffing and green beans. Mom mashed the potatoes. Last but not least, Judy and Stink put out the popcorn.

In no time, the Moodys sat down to Thanksgiving dinner. The room got quiet as they munched away on turkey dogs.

"Turkey dogs are good," said Stink.

"A-*maize*-ing!" said Judy, taking a big bite.

"Nothing beats good old beans and franks," said Dad.

"Happy *Franks*giving!" Judy said. Stink almost spit out his turkey dog.

"Now let's each say something we're thankful for," said Judy.

"Great idea," said Grandma Lou. They went around the table. Grandma Lou and

Mom and Dad said they were thankful for mushy stuff (family) and boring stuff (health).

Then it was Judy's turn. "I'm thankful to Sarah Josepha Hale for inventing Thanksgiving. And I'm thankful that my wishbone wish came true. I mean, especially since it was just a puny old chicken wishbone."

"That's two thankfuls," said Stink. "Do I get two, too?"

"Sure," said Grandma Lou.

"I'm thankful I'm not a turkey," said Stink.

"Who said you're not a turkey?" Judy teased.

The room got quiet again. "Stink, we're

waiting," said Judy. "What's your second thankful? Thankful Number Two."

"Oh, yeah. I'm thankful that Judy brought her entire wishbone collection. Because . . . what would Thanksgiving be without a wishbone?" He elbowed Judy. "Hint, hint."

"No way, Stinker," said Judy.

Stink ran and grabbed the shoe box full of wishbones anyway. He held it out to Judy. "I'm thankful that Judy is going to let me make a wish on one of her for-real turkey wishbones."

"Okay, okay!" said Judy. She reached in and pulled out a beauty. A real turkey-not-chicken wishbone.

Judy held on to one end of the wishbone.

She closed her eyes. Stink took hold of the other end.

"Make a wish, Stink," said Judy.

Judy made a wishbone wish, secretly and to herself. Stink closed his eyes and made a wish, too.

SNAP!

"I win!" yelled Stink. "I got the bigger half. I win, I win, I win."

"What did you wish for, Stink?"

"I wished that I'd win the wishbone wish."

"That's not a real wish, Stink."

"Ya-huh! It already came true. I won, didn't I?" He zoomed around the room. Mom, Dad, and Grandma Lou couldn't help laughing.

111

"This is the best first Thanksgiving ever!" said Stink.

"For your information, Stink, the first Thanksgiving was in 1621," Judy told him.

"I know, but this is *our* first of two Thanksgivings. We get to have our second Thanksgiving tomorrow. Right, Grandma Lou?"

"Right!" said Grandma Lou.

"Everybody knows that two Thanksgivings are better than one," said Judy.

Amazing facts about the real Sarah Josepha Hale

- Sarah J. loved to read when she was a child. Even when she grew up, she read for TWO HOURS every single night, from 8:00 to 10:00 P.M.

- Think the word *underwear* is embarrassing? So did Sarah J., so she popularized use of the word *lingerie* to refer to undergarments instead. *Ooh-la-la!*

- When Thomas Edison invented the phonograph, the first human speech he ever recorded was someone reciting the opening lines of "Mary's Lamb," a poem that Sarah J. had written. (By the way, that rhyme is now called "Mary Had a Little Lamb." Maybe you've heard of it?)

- Next time you swing on a swing or slide down a slide, you can thank Sarah J. She was the one who came up with the idea of playgrounds for kids.

- Sarah J. believed in education and exercise for girls. Things she did NOT believe in:
  1. fancy clothes
  2. spanking
  3. eating pie for breakfast

- *Same-same!* Just like Judy Moody, Sarah J. was a big supporter of Elizabeth Blackwell, First Woman Doctor, and her right to attend medical school.

- Sarah J. was the first woman magazine editor in America.

- Sarah J. was friends with Lydia Maria Child, the person who wrote "Over the River and Through the Wood," the most famous American Thanksgiving poem ever!

- Sarah J. wasn't afraid to speak her mind. She wrote letters to presidents Zachary Taylor, Millard Fillmore, Franklin Pierce, and James Buchanan, asking each of them to declare a Thanksgiving holiday. They said *No, No, No,* and *No.* She didn't give up! On September 28, 1863, Sarah J. wrote a letter to President Abraham Lincoln asking him to proclaim the last Thursday in November as an annual national day of Thanksgiving. He said *Yes!* Don't believe it? You can read the for-real letter that Sarah wrote to President Lincoln at the Library of Congress (loc.gov).